To Harold,

who makes my heart dance

—S.H.

To a couple of sillyheads,

Bridget and Alanna

DANCING

by **Sarah Hager**

illustrated by **Kelly Murphy**

HarperCollinsPublishers

matilda

DANCING Matilda
DANCES out of bed,
DANCES to the drumbeat
DANCING in her head!

DANCES with her SHOES—
DANCES with her SHIRT—

DANCES down to breakfast

in her TUTU SKIRT!

DANCE, Miss Matilda! DANCE, Miss Matilda!
DANCE and DANCE and—

DANCING Matilda
DANCES for a kiss—

DANCES for a bear hug—

OOPS!

—Daddy MISSED!

DANCES with a BOWL—

DANCES with a CUP—

DANCES when her mommy

says to MOP THAT UP!

DANCE, Miss Matilda! DANCE, Miss Matilda!

DANCE and DANCE

and DANCE and—

DANCING Matilda,
DANCING queen,
DANCES to the sloshing
of the washing machine!

DANCES like a BUTTERFLY—
DANCES like a BRIDE—

DANCES till her daddy says to DANCE OUTSIDE!

DANCE, Miss Matilda! DANCE, Miss Matilda!
DANCE and DANCE
and DANCE and DANCE and—

DANCING Matilda
DANCES down the stairs,

DANCES in the mud—

DANCES when the mail comes BOUNCING PAST,

DANCES till she's dizzy
'cause she DANCED SO FAST!

DANCE, Miss Matilda! DANCE, Miss Matilda!
DANCE and DANCE

and DANCE and DANCE and DANCE and

DANCING Matilda—Go, Girl, GO!
DANCES like the traffic cop—
blow, blow, BLOW!

DANCES in the BARBERSHOP!

DANCES home for dinner—

——time to DANCE a little MORE!

DANCE, Miss Matilda! DANCE, Miss Matilda!

DANCE and DANCE

and DANCE and DANCE

and DANCE and

DANCE and —

DANCING Matilda
DANCES in her socks,
KICKING to the ticking
of the GRAND-DADDY CLOCK!

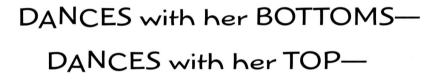

DANCES with her BOTTOMS—
DANCES with her TOP—

DANCES on her bed

till her mommy says,

DANCE, Miss Matilda! DANCE, Miss Matilda!

DANCE and

DANCE

and DANCE

and

DANCE and

DANCE and DANCE and DANCE and DANCE, Miss Matilda!

DANCING Matilda's
DANCING to the beat,

but only in her dreams, 'cause

Matilda's
fast
asleep.

DANCE, Miss Matilda!

DANCE, Miss Matilda!

DANCE and DANCE and DANCE,

Miss Matilda!

DANCE, Miss Matilda!

DANCE, Miss Matilda!

DANCE and DANCE and DANCE,

Miss Matilda!

Library of Congress Cataloging-in-Publication Data

Hager, Sarah.

Dancing Matilda / by Sarah Hager ; illustrated by Kelly Murphy. — 1st ed.

p.   cm.

Summary: Matilda dances through every part of her day.

ISBN 0-06-051452-3 — ISBN 0-06-051453-1 (lib. bdg.)

[1. Dance—Fiction.   2. Stories in rhyme.]   I. Murphy, Kelly, ill.   II. Title.

PZ8.3.H1192Dan   2005   2004004575

[E]—dc22

Typography by Martha Rago

1 2 3 4 5 6 7 8 9 10

❖

First Edition